SLAUGHTER

Hildyard

ISBN: 978-1-913642-41-9

The author has asserted their right to be identified as the author of this Work in accordance with the Copyright, Designs and Patents Act 1988

Book designed by Aaron Kent

Edited by Aaron Kent

Broken Sleep Books (2021), Talgarreg, Wales

Contents

Slaughter

Rosanna Hildyard

Offcomers

Ravenseat, North Yorkshire.
2001

I wake up because he is not snoring.

I turn my head. Still dark outside, the moon resting on the moor like a fingernail clipping. His head is on the pillow beside me, and I can see the gleam of his eyeballs. When his voice rasps, it is a shock.

What if we get it, he says.

I blink and mumble. We won't, I say. It won't get as far as us, don't worry.

I'm not worried about *us*, he says, and he spits the *us*. I'm thinking about those fucking tourists down in Catterick. Fucking offcomers.

He is talking about the farmer he pays to shelter our sheep in the valley over winter. It is spring now, lambing time and time for our eight hundred pure-bred Swaledale ewes to come back to the uplands, with us. But we've just heard that all movement of animals is banned until the foot-and-mouth is over.

His tone sends a chill down my spine. Farmers don't talk about other farmers in that way. They're not just colleagues; they are allies in the same fight. No matter how much he might scorn or whinge about his neighbours, he does it with a grudging respect.

This sounds different. They best take care of them, he says, and I know that note of warning, and I feel it in the pit of my stomach: bad things lie ahead in the Catterick farmer's future. Then he rolls onto his side, his back rising up before me, and I can no longer see his open eyes.

I close my own eyes and try not to think of the pigs in the Essex abattoir, hanging dead and cold with blisters on their lip-less mouths. The first cases in England. They say it's spreading north. I wonder how it is that I can't just reach out and touch him – *hey, are you awake?* – and yet I am as unable to do that as if I were paralysed, or frozen, or something was holding my arms behind my back and pinning me down.

I open my eyes again. The moon looks like a thin, curved smile.

*

Sky's all pearly outside next morning, when I get up at six. Place my feet carefully as I go down the bare wood of the stairs, so as not to slip and make noise over his radio. The house is more lived-in than it was last year, when I moved in, but it's still what some people – people who don't get us – might call empty. But it's like he says: we don't need flowery things when all we do here is grab a bite of food, and sleep. Well, OK, I took up the carpet with a pair of shears, when I decided I was here for good, and he let me strip the yellowy, smoke-stained wallpaper – but no more.

I am still thinking about how it was as I cross the stone flags of the kitchen and reach the back door. I pull on overalls on, my own breath curling out before me as I fumble boots on. Smells of dogshite.

Outside, there is a streak of hot pink at the horizon. Shepherd's warning, I think, and mind to check the horoscope later, crossing my fingers in the meantime to ward off bad luck. Himself and the dogs are already down by the cattle grid. They are barking, and the quad bike is revving, and he is shouting at the both of them. Come by Floss; Sky, come by. And then a yell back up to me. Come on, then.

He revs the quad bike, not looking back. What am I waiting for? He is going out, onto the moor, when we have the scant hundred older sheep we kept with us, and no lambs.

I pull my hood up and follow him. Onto the moor, where only curlews rise and sing.

*

When I was training as a florist, back when I lived with my dad, my boss told me about shipments of exotic flowers carrying stowaways. Tarantulas, poisonous red ants, Black Widows, she'd said, walking her dirty fingernails over the counter. They invade the ecosystem and have no predators. I imagined it: unrolling brown paper on your kitchen table, all a-crackle, when out of the stems squirms some fat, boneless, black thing that has scuttled off before you can move a muscle. And, later, you're trousers-down on the bog or sweating over your onions when you feel a cold snip at your ankle... And that's it, for you.

I told him about the spiders in flowers and he snorted. That's how diseases spread! I said. Maybe there are sheep ticks, or flies, or something!

We were sitting on the sofa. He was shovelling in his baked beans and I was screwed up in a corner, toothing the chocolate off the sides of a Blue Riband and trying not to shiver. Fuck that, he said. Be easy enough if it was a matter of catching a couple of spiders.

You what? I said. Have you ever tried to catch a spider?

He didn't even bother to look up from scraping the baked bean tin. They're bloody great big things, he said. This is a virus. It's carried on the wind.

His brow started going all creased as he stared down into the tin. Then he shook his head abruptly, and cleared his throat. Nineteen-sixty-seven, he said. It got blown northwards by the wind. And in nineteen-eighty it got blown onto the Isle of Wight, from France. It's a windborne virus. But it can be carried on cars, clothes, shoes – those bloody hikers, offlanders, they don't belong here. That's why they've locked the Coast to Coast path down so fast, this time.

He stopped, tipped his head back and shook the last dregs of juice from the tin. I watched his Adam's apple bobbing up and one small orange drip trickling down his beard. He put the can down, sighed and rubbed his jaw, apparently without noticing. Windborne? Wasn't that what people thought in, like, medieval times? I thought. He had to be kidding.

I felt suddenly starving for baked beans, put down my gnawed chocolate bar and got up, glancing at the grey hairs in his beard as I did. Windborne? He was obviously desperate. He'd left school years ago; he needed to have an explanation, I thought. He was older than me, after all.

But that was in late March, and as we watched the news each night, I began to feel a creeping suspicion. It was like an invisible giant was stamping north, county by county: Devon, Wales, one quick stride up into Lancashire, coming for us. We watched its footsteps tracking up the country, and my old world – Tesco and schoolfriends having babies, Afghanistan on TV and catching the bus to town – they just bled away.

And when I realized that's what it was – coming for us – I felt relief, deep down in my gut. I've come to realise that's what you feel, when the worst happens: relief. You should have known. You were right, that plague would descend; and on you, of all people. You knew what you always feared would come to be.

The news didn't stop mentioning it. Far from it; they sounded less and less alarmed, the newsreaders' voices deepening into a kind of warm, resigned apology. *And in the North, the Foot and Mouth crisis continues. Blair talks with… In Cumbria alone…* Decontamination zone. Carcasses. Contiguous cull. Bonfire.

Like him, I started arriving breathlessly for the next update every few hours, hanging back in the doorway so I didn't disturb as he leant over the radio. But I couldn't help it. What is Type O? I'd blurt out. Or: isn't that south of us? No, that's not south, he'd say. Didn't you hear him say there was an outbreak in Berwick, as well? Fool, it's not south of us.

He'd roll his eyes, and turn away. His forehead seemed to be growing like a limestone cliff, those ploughed furrows in his forehead deepening. I'd watch as his massive back disappeared outside, and I'd be left alone, with the shadows creeping around me and only the sound of the wind on the grass like laughter in my ears.

*

I am not a real farmer, like him. The first time I saw this place, I was doing a delivery for my dad. I was only eighteen and could barely drive, but my dad dealt in things that fell off the backs of lorries, as he put it, and wasn't much bothered about shoulds and couldn'ts. Drop this load off at Skabbawath, will you? he said, one winter morning as he sat like a fat old woodlouse curled up in his chair. Everyone's bloody fucked me over, again. I don't know why everything's against me. Sod's Law, whatever I try to do…

He whined on about this for a bit, about how the whole world turned just to spite him, bringing up my mum again, then sighed piteously as he wound round to the point … Least *you* could do is help your dad out, once in a while, all right?

OK, Dad, I said, pushing my hair off my face. Skabba-where?

It was all right, the florists. People never ordered more than the most basic type of bouquet. I spent a lot of time spray-painting chairs gold for my old schoolfriends' weddings. Not much point getting your diploma, eh, pet! my old boss used to cackle. But it was OK. I liked the idea of it, I think. Being there at the most meaningful rituals of people's whole lives, that kind of thing. I'd end up like my boss, I sort of vaguely thought. A bit weird, probably with bad teeth, but at least not having a spray-painted wedding or getting into the same kind of mess my mum and dad had. They thought they could squeeze life like a lemon in their fists, and look where that had gone and got them. Her, running off to Manchester in a desperate game of catch-up with her youth, ending up turning tricks in Canal Street, if my dad were to be believed. And him, chairbound in a ground-floor flat, railing that the politicians were out to get him, and none of it was fair.

What neither of them ever worked out is that you can't demand happiness of life. The world is hard, and you're a nothing, and you have to bend yourself to forces that you can't fight. Accept that you're weak, and only then will you be happy. They never realised, it can be sort of good, giving in.

I thought that the florists was what I was meant for. But fate, she turns back on herself and spirits you away in a direction you'd never have thought of, and you can't do anything more than be carried along by her flow.

My dad said he'd sold a load of scrap iron to a farmer and hadn't reckoned on how he'd get it to the farm, which was miles up the Dales somewhere. Fucked me right over, he said. So you can do it. A'right?

Yeah, dad, I said. Course.

The journey took hours. From the flat, I drove to Scotch Corner and onto the motorway, turned off and drove for a while through a flat sprawl of estates and barracks at the army garrison, drove through a maze of cul-de sacs, drove twice round a roundabout before I worked out where I was, and then suddenly I was driving up on the moorside, entirely alone. A single road wound alongside a river the colour of stewed tea, through meadows dotted with crumbling barns. Below me, stunted little trees pressed in over the water; and above, the wide expanse of heather and gold sky.

I drove on, keeping my eyes peeled for Skabbawath. But no turn-offs, just those eyeless barns and the ruins of what looked like mines. There were no people. It was built of simple forces. The bog against the sucking water. The sun fighting the wind. The colours all bright. Green, purple, yellow, brown.

At one point, I stopped. I'd leant out of the window and the wind sucked the breath right out of me. For the first time since I'd left my dad and the sickly warmth of the florists, I didn't feel anxious. This harsh, sharp landscape didn't bother about me. I may as well have been invisible. There is something good about feeling small.

Light gradually leaked out of the valley as I drove, the high walls of the valley cupped against the sun. One, then two hours passed. And then, just as I was growing uneasy, a sign flashed up in front of me. An actual sign: a Black Sheep Brewery advert, popping up from nowhere. Still people, then, I thought, slowing down. What sort of person could live out here, on the knife edge of the world?

TAN HILL INN:
'THE HIGHEST PUB IN ENGLAND!'
ACCOMODATION MORNING COFFEE & MEALS
RUSTIC BARN
WEDDING LICENSES

And a few miles after that, there was a white board on the verge, roughly painted with reddish letters: S CABBA-WATH FARM, and a gravel track leading away from the sign.

It was right on the top of the dale. Nothing but cold bog and tussocks of grass, A few pinpricks of light in the distance the nearest village.

When my car finally scraped complainingly into the foldyard at twilight, there was a huge man bending over something there. As he straightened up and turned, I felt a rush of weakness all down my body. Tall, but stooped. Black curling hair over most of his face and neck. Iron blue lines in a waving pattern down his arms.

I stuck my head out. I'm Metcalfe's daughter, I said, and the daring was so unlike me that I knew something was happening. I've got half a barn in my car for you, will you give us a hand?

He must've been twice my age. The future I'd seen myself in melted off like morning mist and I didn't even notice. Wedding licenses – I realised it must have been yet another omen I'd ignored. It was all significant: this weird place had given me something better to serve; better than my dad. Later, I thought it was as if I was that piece of corrugated iron, and he was the North Pole.

Did you sell me? I asked my dad, when I got back home late that night. You what? he said. Sell me, I said. I'm not being funny. I feel like I've been picked up and moved from one place to another.

My dad scratched his head and gave a high, little giggle. You say some bloody weird stuff sometimes, he said. Sell you, to that mad gadgie? Mind you, least you're not going round trapping some poor decent fella, like your mother... An't I always saying it, what a fucked-up mind you have? Must be from your mother.

Well, I dunno, I said, rubbing my nose. I know it sounds stupid... I just felt like I was meant to go to that place. Like, there's some larger force, up there.

I could see my dad's eyes popping out – *what, like G-O-D?* – and he almost actually heaved himself up and out of his chair, almost trippng over his own trainers in his haste to get to the kitchen. Ignore it, shove it away. That was always his way of pretending he had some control over the world.

*

I've learned a lot since I came here. How to bottlefeed a lamb, how to birth a lamb, how to drench a ewe, how to make fire out of a lighter and some miniscule scraps of old receipts, on a bog, when it's raining. But also stuff like: there are very few things you mind, if you have plenty to keep you busy. If you'd asked me when I was living with my dad, I would've said I wouldn't like to eat only tinned food, or sleep on a damp and mouldy mattress, in a room that flaked plaster and birdshit. But if you come in dead tired after a day's lambing or fencing, you don't mind if the sofa you flop down on is a bit mucky. If there's a job to do and you've got to do it, because it could mean life or death, for the animals. Life, death, simple. It's more meaningful than the florists. Much better than my dad's.

After I'd dropped off the iron, he rang my dad and asked for me. I listened through the door, and felt something twist in the pit of my stomach, because I'd *known* he would call. I really had. I can tell these things. Sometimes.

*

Since February, there are signs all over the place:

THE FOOT AND MOUTH DISEASE (AMENDMENT) (ENGLAND) ORDER 2001
ENTRY ONTO THIS LAND IS PROHIBITED
ALL PUBLIC FOOTPATHS AND RIGHTS OF WAY ARE CLOSED.

Every time I see one of them, I mentally read it in Trevor Marsden's voice, because he photocopied and laminated the signs for us, and because Trevor's natural way of talking is to underline a lot of words.

Trev farms nearer town. He did us a favour.

Fucking offcomers, he had said this morning.

I have never seen him so weak, so much looking for something to blame.

*

Now we are roaring back down the moorside, me clinging on the back of the quad bike. Foddering has not taken long, because we only have the hundred or so ewes we kept up on the farm with us. Sent the other eight hundred to winter in Catterick, like every year. Hill farmers send their young breeders down-dale around about November time, and bring them back onto the hills for lambing in late March. He pays the farmers in Catterick so much, per head: heads he's held in his own hands.

When I'd said that last bit, he'd grunted and said rubbish, he'd slaughter them himself if he needed to. But you do love them, even if you pretend you don't, I said. You're got a deep connection with them. You birth 'em. It's symbolic.

On the quad bike, I'm spreadeagled against his back. He is thin, I can feel it, and feel bad about it. I'd like to cook more than just tinned stuff and lasagne from all our frozen mutton. We can't grow vegetables, he says it's too cold. I tried buying bread mixes so we could have fresh bread, but they got weevils. I swore, last time I opened a packet and saw their little black slimespots in my flour. What's that? he said. Bastards in my bread mix! I said. Just buy bread and stick it in't freezer, he said. And when I thought about it, I realised he was right. He is always right. I gave way to nature and stopped trying to force an allotment on the heaf.

To bring in 2001, we had beers by the fire. Flames flickering over his face when he said, out of nowhere: You think it's all some kind of magical wilderness, here, don't you? Well, it's not natural, even if it might look it. It's centuries of hill farmers have shaped this land. Men just like me.

I remember looking into the fire and trying to hide a smile. Yeah, but look at him: earth caked into the creases of his elbows, bones like flint. Eejit, I thought. You're just one more part of this place, another cog in the ecosystem, as much as the birds are. Even if you like to pretend you're the big man in charge.

Grouse shooting, sheep cropping the pasture, us humans protecting the peat and the active bogs, he said, light playing across the shadow in his cheek. Sphagum mosses, he said. We keep the balance. Farmers have created this environment, here. And then those bloody offcomers come walking over our fields…

How do you know about active bogs? I said, flicking my hair back, and I guess my mouth had smiled or I'd sounded sarcastic, or something, because he stood up so fast his chair smashed onto the kitchen flags.

That was one of the early points on the learning curve. I should've been more careful. I should've paid attention to what I was saying. Those who think themselves high and mighty might do well to remember, pride comes before a fall.

I should've tried harder to explain that to him.

*

So, we are roaring back down. I'm always terrified we'll hear a crunched-off squawk below us from one of the curlews that nest on the ground, up here. They didn't evolve to deal with humans. Or quad bikes.

When we arrive back at the farm, the phone is ringing inside. Fuck! he shouts, and is already leaping off the bike and sprinting through the door, sending me lurching forward, scrabbling to turn the engine off. Is it the Catterick farm? I call, following him into the gloomy sitting room.

He is perched on the sofa, curled over the phone and looking in pain. Yes, he grunts. Yes, I understand. All right. And you're sure it'd be no use for us to come down? Aye, we've been told to stay put, I just thought… Aye. No. Well, let us know. He puts the receiver down and looks up at me with eyes all sad and Bambi-like.

No news is good news, I try.

His face twists. Fuck you, he snarls, and stamps out, shoulders sunk, looking utterly defeated. In his big brown coat, he looks like a shambling collection of rocks, I think, and immediately an image springs up, of the rough limestone cobbles that lie jumbled on the peaty riverbed.

I can see it so clearly: the water rushing over. A vision?

I swallow, then run after him. Outside, he is standing and staring up into the sky, with our own Sky and Floss circling his ankles.

I try. We'll get compensation, I say. If the Catterick farmer gets told to cull them.

Fuck compensation, he says. I own those sheep, they can't just – fucking – shooting them! Those sheep have been bred here for fucking years!

He takes a step back, still gazing up at the blue. Do you hear that? he shouts. We've been here fucking years! And he staggers, nearly falling onto the muck of the foldyard. It's OK, I say. No, it's not, he says. I'm in charge, here. His chin suddenly snaps down, and he looks at me with focus. I know that look, and step back. But I know there is no use fighting. I do not run.

*

Later, back in the kitchen. The fridge is cold against my cheekbone.

Roll my head against it: up to forehead and back down again: stinging hot, wet, turning cold. Out of the corner of my eye, I notice Sky slinking in.

Sky, I say. Get out.

Our two dogs have short, sharp names, to be called by. They are hill dogs, not inside dogs. Sky is well aware that working dogs shouldn't be inside.

There is a warm, soft gap between Sky's ribs, and a particular kind of huffing whine she gives as the toe of my boot connects, pushing sharply up into it. I feel better. Her black lips roll back and her tongue dangles. Now out, I say. I touch my sore forehead and swelling cheek, quickly.

*

Wet heath, dry heath, blanket bog, curlew, black grouse, ring ouzel, field vole, merlin, short-eared owl, adder, red grouse, golden plover, sundew, meadow pipit, hen harrier, tenant farmer.

When I am upset, I list the things that do not change.

He huddles over the phone, ringing the Catterick farm. Hello? You again? Look, we'll call if… Yeah, but you won't just cull 'em without asking, right? You'll ask me first, right?

The sigh from the other end. …Mate. If the army turns up… You know there's nothing we can do.

Then he tries Tan Hill, punching his finger into the plastic buttons as if he's trying to start a fight with them. He dials again and again, perched on the arm of the sofa or pacing the gloomy room while outside the sun smiles over the April and May evenings, and each evening I go into the kitchen and heat up a tin of Heinz Big Soup for him so he'll eat something. It smells and looks like dog food, lumps slopping brownishly from the tin. I find myself glancing out of the window uncomfortably, as if something's watching what we eat. He'd call me stupid. But we must be doing something wrong.

There's always something you should be watching out for.

Soup's up, I shout, and carry it to him with a spoon standing up in it and a grin plastered on my face.

*

One day. Pearly early, I walk down to the river, heading through the meadows. There's a brisk breeze and clouds drift quickly across the sun, so that the bright spring colours all around me are continually flashing bright and then leaching out into shadow. The meadow is wet with dew, the birds are twittering fit to burst and I can almost feel the leaves photosynthesizing, the grass pushing up and up and up like greeny tendons of muscle without the sheep to crop it down. Normally, this time of year, there would be lambs gambolling everywhere.

I chuck some round pebbles in the waterfall and ask it to let us keep our flock. Let us keep them, please. We're part of this world, too. I shut my eyes and think of last spring, my first here. The tiny woollen scraps with pipe-cleaner legs skittering around everywhere. The mothers lying down to give birth in the lush grass, groaning, and the dogs sniffing at placentas that we'd kicked into the hedges. It was all life. And I felt one with it, not swept up in a terrible current and struggling against it, as now.

I hear water clucking along. Trees sighing. Please, I say, and hear my own voice: a pathetic cheep. Before my mother left, she used to say that she didn't know why I was such a wimp, why I let people boss me around all the time. Don't be such a bloody creep, she said. Yes, mum, I said, and prayed that she'd go away, and she did, she went looking for something better and left me with my dad. I'd tempted fate. There's always something you've done. Cross your fingers and don't step on the cracks; take all the care you possibly can.

I take a deep breath, then open my eyes and look around for the moon, until I find it perched – scrap of tracing-paper – on the brow of the hill.

*

When I arrive back, after splashing my wellies in the buckets of yellow disinfectant we keep at the gates, he is sitting in the dark by the telephone. I ask if there's been any news, and he shakes his head. But Marsden saw a lorry dripping today, he says. His fingers are flexing – like massive, hairy spiders, I think – otherwise, he is completely still. And Peacock's blocked his road with a trailer's worth of boulders, he says. Not even a fucking tank could get through to his flock. Maybe I'll do that.

My dad calls, awkwardly, to tell me he's heard rumours it's arrived in the north. We're fine, I tell him before he can explain why he can't come to get me. Don't come: you'd have to disinfect all your clothes. Humans can't get it, so we're fine.

*

April. It's only been a few weeks – two months – and our life is bounded by it. Is that an ulcer! he says, and snatches in terror at the sheep's head. But these ewes we kept up with us are only the old matriarchs, and long since barren. Still, he rounds them up, protesting, inside the barn, where he checks each jaw obsessively – red spittle? A blister? I pick my nails and mentally calculate the natural things he must've killed, each year. Spraying meadows. Crushing curlew eggs. Tipping rubbish in the river. I can practically feel the back of my neck prickling, like something's watching. Please, I think.

Only yesterday, one of the Ministers had said, *We're finally getting on top of the disease.* And then it goes and jumps to another farm, as the radio has just told us, forty miles distant from any other case. Like magic, clearly. Like a curse, rising up through the earth. He's right; it would be easier if it was locusts or flies or spiders stripping this land to desert, but when I look around and see the bright April sun, tawny grass, babbling beck all unbothered and untouched, doesn't that just prove all the more that it's us that this disease is getting at? It's skimming us off the land like scum off cheese.

Why do you think it's only pigs and sheep and cows? I ask, slyly. And not birds or voles, or badgers?

He yanks a staple out of a post. Years of work! he says, abruptly. Compensation? It's taken me ten years to build up this flock; keep 'em healthy in this blasted bleak place, lamb 'em, shear 'em. Spend six weeks every year dragging lambs out of ewes legs-first. Split up triplets so the mothers don't die. Our herd, that's down at Catterick, has been bred on this land for generations. Centuries. They're pure Swaledales. A couple of fucking grand?

I remember him showing me last year's triplets. I had stood beside him, by the incubators in the barn, as he showed me the lone lambs that had to be removed from their mothers. I take care of my flock, he told me, proudly, showing me the weak lambs. One bleated pitifully, then forced its black nose into my hand with surprising strength. I'd lay down and they could walk all over me, he'd said, chuckling. I watched him, veins flexing in his arms, as he knelt in the straw and fed them.

Look, I say now, daringly. Look. What if it doesn't stop? Maybe you should think of something else – if we can't farm.

I am stumbling over my own words. But the moon. That something, watching.

This land has had enough of us, I say. All the animals dying, I say. They're domestic animals, farm animals. Can't you see? This place has had enough of humans. There's something here stopping us – I know it sounds crazy –

And it's like one minute he is staring at me with his hands by his side, the next, I am flying backwards. For a millisecond I think wildly: Ha, missed. And then the pain collides into my skull and I am lying in the mud with face thrumming and my brain feeling rearranged.

Don't talk crap, he says, standing over me with fists dangling uselessly. He pauses and I see him swallow. I'd as soon you got it, he says. I've spent as long caring for you as I have for these lambs. I'm bloody responsible for the lot of you, a fucking teenager and a herd, aren't I?

I shrug, and shuffle deeper into my hooded jacket like an earthworm, because what else can I do.

Eventually he says: I'm fucking going down there and getting them! and stamps off.

He doesn't. He goes inside, and I hear the TV buzz on. I lie on my back like the pig in shit I am, and look at the sky. And I can't help it – even though I understand, even though I know he is feeling weak and powerless and he is the kind of man who can't bear to be doing nothing – tears spring to my eyes and I hate him. Mud on my teeth as I spit out aloud what I am thinking: *You should be lying here, begging, too.*

*

He phones, he broods over his remaining sheep, his hands twitch, longing for something to fill them. I watch him and think of rotting scabs on hooves. The dogs' black, mirrored eyes watch him and me.

*

We have no curtains, and so I open my eyes straight to the sky. Pearl, or lilies, or dirty wool. It is May, now; it must be well past seven. Why am I so late to wake up?

I lie on my back and stare at the cracks in the ceiling. All is still: that is what has woken me.

I follow the silence downstairs. Down, slowly on each step so they don't creak over the radio and cause him to yell. Cross the stone flags, and then I nearly have a heart attack, because Sky rises silently from where she has been lying by the stove. Now then, girl, I say. Her shoulder nubs rise, and her black lip. I take a quick look at the phone behind her, and see that the red light is flashing: someone has left a voicemail.

Catterick? A million and one thoughts flash through my head. You should be outside, I hurl at Sky, and push past her.

Not by the cattle grid, the quad bike is still parked and so are the cars. I stand, staring blankly around. He can't have gone down there. So, what was the message?

(The spider, biting when you least expect it –)

And then I get it. And I turn, slipping on the mud, to the closed bar. Shuttered up. Black-clad, iron roof.

I can almost see his face, his hands bottlefeeding a lamb, his empty hands flexing, yesterday. And I know what is in there, now; I can smell it: something sweetish, and gunsmoke hanging in the air, and I can feel that inside there is only silence and stillness.

And an electric buzz goes down my spine, and I can feel it, something, hanging in the roiling sky and watching me, alone on this blasted moor.

I vibrate for a second, panicking. If I get in the car, that's it: I can't just drive back in here. The roads are all blocked. A vision of my dad, sunk in his chair complaining, swims into my mind, and I feel the usual surge of pity and pointless rage, and I know, right to the very marrow of my bones, that I don't want to go back to that little life where everything was grey and unclear and I couldn't see which path to follow, not as ordered and clear and simple as it is here.

But the blocked roads. The infection. The barn. The infection. The barn. I cannot go inside the barn.

And I feel like I am stuck fast, in a web he spun for us, and cannot move either way. I cannot, cannot go inside the barn.

A lone bark: Floss has emerged from the house, and lopes out, sniffing at the air. She doesn't even look at me; us humans are already something of the past, to her. Windborne and blown away by winter.

I look at the sky. Already blue, and a curlew spiralling there, and it is a sign if there ever was one, and so I turn from this wild place, this place of ruined barns and lead mines, speechless fields and derelict farms; this place that humans must always leave, and I run to the car.

Outside Are The Dogs

She arrived in a taxi that could've fitted seven people in it, including the driver. He watched it winding down the lane towards him, a little flag of St George attached to the aerial, and couldn't help thinking, what a waste of all that extra space. There were plenty of things he and Da could have done with from the big town – a few sacks of chickenfeed, or stakes, or the plough coulter. But that was not exactly the kind of thing you could ask when a woman like this came to live with you the first time.

When the taxi pulled up in front of the bungalow and the engine died, she waited for him to open the door before she stuck her head out, blinking. Like a battery chicken brought into daylight, he thought, proudly. Set free. She stepped out into the yard and shaded her eyes to look around as the taxi driver brought her baggage. Yes, only one suitcase – and he'd barely call it that, such a battered old thing.

'Is this the back?' she said. He didn't know what she meant, so he didn't bother answering. She looked at the heap of tyres, the chickens, the breezeblocks that separated the yard from the field. She turned and looked at the bungalow. 'Oh,' she said. 'How old is it?' His father built it for him, he told her. Knocked down the old barn the farmhands used to sleep in, which was only a bothy anyway.

'A what?' she said. He said nothing, watching her pink-dimpled elbows move up and down. She didn't wait for him to speak, anyway. 'The way you talked about it,' she said, 'made it sound... Well, you said it was old.'

'Oh, aye, it's an old farm,' he said, lifting a hand westwards, to the farmhouse where his parents lived.

'Oh,' she said. 'I thought you meant – well, I didn't expect... I thought perhaps Victorian, or. At least...'

She stood still. Her hand was still gracefully upraised, her red hair looped over her shoulders in an intricately scruffy arrangement. She was wearing some kind of green, silky thing, with flowers embroidered on the shoulders. Not exactly the kind of gear people wore round here. Mostly, that was uniforms – supermarket tabards, army camouflage, the tattered waxed coats of shooters and farmers – and, after work, fleece. It was cold, round here. Well, never mind: she was certainly what his father would call a 'fine-looking lass'. He'd done his parents proud. Done the farm proud.

He smiled. 'Let's be getting inside, shall we?'

*

They had met on a blind date in the big town. 'High time you got a woman,' his ma had said one night, when he was over at theirs for dinner. She was a dry woman, his ma; dry as dust, and at first he wasn't sure if she was joking. He was in the middle of stuffing in a loaded spoonful of shepherd's pie, mouth full. 'You'll be running this farm one day,' she'd said, narrowing her eyes at him. 'A woman's touch, what you need. You've got rid of those spots you had, naw. Any hinny would be grateful,' and he'd chewed and swallowed, knowing there was no use in answering back, even if he'd cared to.

He'd looked in the mirror that night. Gingery beard, the family nose, blue eyes; a little watery, perhaps. Face a little young, if it wasn't for the scanty beard covering the acne scars. But he was tall, if stooped, and his freckled arms were strong. Girls liked that, didn't they? The couple of girls he'd had so far – Kerry, Lucy – had never complained. He rubbed his stubble and gave himself a bare-teethed smile.

So he'd called a couple of people, to ask them if they knew a lass. And at last: 'I know just the one,' said an old friend of his, and told him he had a cousin just moved back home. 'A great girl, really great,' the friend had said. 'Went to uni down South; been travelling ever since. Fun-lover, backpacking. Now, at the last minute, decides she'd better come home and settle down, afore it's too late. Wants a bairn. Women, eh? Always the same story!'

And on Friday night, after leaving the supermarket, he changed out of his work fleece in the car and drove the hour and a half down the motorway to the town.

He has always found speaking to others difficult. The kids used to tease him at school; would laugh at his stronger accent, and the weird old words his parents used. 'Dee'n't for 'didn't', 'wick' for 'alive', 'tha'sen' for 'yourself'. They actually said: 'eh, ba'gum'. The teasing stopped once he grew and gangled a head and shoulders taller than everyone else, but even still. At the supermarket where he works three days a week, he prefers loading and unloading to till service. He hates talking. The words seem rough like a mouthful of loose teeth in his mouth, and they clatter out to land like a handful of gravel on the ground.

They ate in a tiny, red-painted restaurant that he was sure had used to be a takeaway. Didn't he remember getting chips here with the lads, years ago? But it was a good year or more since he'd been out in the big town. These days, after work, he just wanted to slump in front of the telly. A quiet life, that was what his parents liked, and so it was the same for him. A silent life, to some.

They sat wedged into a matchbox table, barely two feet from where the chef stood humming tunelessly behind a stainless steel countertop. The conversation faltered on its legs, crashed over into silence. He thought of the cow with bloat his dad and he'd been treating last week, and tried surreptitiously to wipe his hands on the paper tablecloth. It jerked towards him, and her perfect eyebrows shot up to her hairline as if connected by a string.

'Well, I've never moved from here,' he said, in desperation. The cow, lying on the floor of the byre, gasping for breath. 'Not like y'self. But in some ways, I think I know the world better for it.' Was that a bored, or an expectant face? 'My family's been here for centuries. Not like we're grand, or owt – my dad used to tell of a branch of the family that married well and moved off, and are lords, now, down south – but, for me, it's being here that's the important thing…' Jesus Christ, what was he talking about? And, more importantly, what in God's name was he going to say next? 'One of my family being here, in perpet – always. Keeping it going, like. For the generations to come. My dad before me and his before, and so on. A duty, I suppose.' His rubbery lips clashed with the rim of the glass. What bollocks was he talking? This wasn't Kerry or Abigail or any of the local girls; the kind he'd grope in a sweaty car after a few pints, and not bring home to meet his mother. This lass was snowy of skin, bare of make-up, a princess. She was a different story altogether.

But she had copied him in taking a sip, and now put her glass down, leaning forward over the gory remains of her spaghetti. She was interested, he belatedly realised. 'I understand,' she said, and he realised she was smiling, too. 'Family, that's what's important. You know, I've been all over, but there's nowhere like here – '

And carried on, going on about the natural warmth of people here, the green-striped local-brand crisp packets and the glittering, dark alleyways of her youth. The conversation allowed itself a breath. He felt the kind of relief he'd felt when his dad had stabbed the cow, with a needle the size of his arm, and she'd deflated, miraculously recovered.

Near the end of dinner, she said that she wanted to settle down, and he accepted this as truth. Why wouldn't he? She believed it herself. 'I'm tired of working, travelling, being alone all the time,' she said confidently, spooning ice cream into her lipsticked mouth. 'I've done that. I'd like to spend more time here. See my mother.' Tea lights spattered her coppery hair with their bobs of light. Later, she would not kiss him, because of the lipstick, but leaned away, laughing.

He went back to his friend's as arranged, so he wouldn't have to drive the hour and a half back home. 'I said, did you like her?'

asked the friend as he shouldered past him and stumbled down the corridor towards the kitchen. His friend followed, jabbering excitedly. 'Well, she was a quiet one when we were teenagers. Brainy, you know. We used to go out sometimes, but she was a bit up herself – kept to her own friends. She's been living on some French island. Africa, or somewhere, with some shitey fella, God knows what for, but now she's back, because she wants her mammy and a bairn, like all the girls she knows from school! Women, eh! It's always the same story. What did you think, then?'

The man gulped and gulped at a pint of icy water. His mouth felt like a clay cave from all that red wine. He caught a sideways glimpse of his friend's eyes, gleaming like spittle, and felt a sudden surge of distaste. Why did people gossip in this fool way? *Only unhappy people talk*, as his mother always said. If you can't think of something nice to say, don't say it. Silence is golden.

He put the glass down abruptly, and pushed past the friend. Paused at the foot of the stairs, thinking to drop a crumb. 'I like a woman who likes to eat,' he said, generously.

And went up to bed, thinking of the melted pistachio ice cream coating the spoon, and her tongue.

*

Things progress well between them. He gets used to pulling on his scratchy woollen shirt in the car after work, then driving down just to eat with her, or take her to a film, or go for a walk around the lit-up streets. She talks and talks, and he finds it delightful, listening to her. She knows so much; she seems to have an opinion or trivia on everything: black-and-white films, the grey stucco-fronted Georgian houses they pass, trends in Chinese food. He drives back late at night – or even in the early hours – he takes care to keep his hands off her. His mother told him. 'I dee'n't want to meet the lassie until she's used to owt. But, for the good Lord's sake – ' jabbing a finger skywards – 'show respect. I don't want to hear bad words said of you.'

She is clever, and he listens. She doesn't seem to mind his long silences: walking round the town, there is always something new for her to flit on to. 'Look, a heron! Wait, your laces are undone.'

Sometimes, their eyes meet, green to blue, and she stops midway through a sentence, and they both smile, apparently in perfect understanding, without words.

It takes only a couple of weeks before he broaches moving her in. To his place, that is: not the farmhouse where his parents live. He'd known it was a bit of a bachelor establishment, and so he'd made some effort to clean up. Moved a whole lot of furniture into the barn and sprayed Febreze in his old wardrobe. He'd strimmed his bit of beard and his hair close to his head, pleased to note as he did so that those scabby red paint-splatters of adolescence had, indeed, mostly faded from his skin; then looked around him. Well, it still wasn't much, but wasn't that exactly why he needed her? A woman's touch, was the phrase, wasn't it?

He'd stood in the kitchen on the day she was due to arrive. A patch of early spring sunlight warming his back, sunlit dust settling on the surfaces. She'd be grateful. His princess. In his telling of the story, he has rescued her.

After the taxi has gone, wobbling into the bungalow in her white high heels, she does her best. She can't help clucking with her tongue at the flocked wallpaper, faded floral sofa. 'Looks untouched since the 1970s!' she says in the front room, and swings around to stare at him. 'Bit bare!' is the kitchen, and he wonders if he shouldn't have cleared it quite so brutally. When she reaches the end of the corridor, he hears her say: 'Is that it?'

But then: 'Well, I never thought this would be easy,' she sighs, when he follows her into the bedroom. She's not looking at him when she says it, and he barely hears her words – almost asks her to speak up, but she's standing at the window and makes such a pretty picture he doesn't want to disturb it. Evening sun spilling across the ploughed fields, her arse in that green silky dress. And then she turns around, saying nothing, and he can finally take her silently in his arms.

*

He recklessly says her he'll buy her anything she wants from town, throws around all sorts of vows and promises. She laughs, and says that all she asks is that he visit his new mother-in-law, once in a while. There's a pause, and then she asks if she'll be going to see his parents, soon? Another pause, and he nods, staring at his orange pint, and her through the glass, mermaid curves . 'Aye, in a while,' he says.

In a while. For now, he doesn't want her and his mother nattering on. Who knows what they'd say? He doesn't want them comparing notes on him. Or, worse, what if they didn't talk? Or if she talked: but about the wrong things?

She'll have to learn how things are, round here. He takes her round the fields. 'See the lambs,' he says, when showing her round the fields; helping her over the gates. 'You can have one, if you like, for your own.'

She pulls her cardigan around her wrists. 'Just like a real farmer's wife,' she says, smiling tightly. He mentally chinks a pint with himself. He was right: a pet lamb is exactly the kind of whimsy she'd think belonged to a farm. He can picture his father and mother with their eyes narrowing and lips thinning, but he's sure she will settle down. He can feel something buoyant building up inside his stomach the longer she's around. This is happiness, he thinks.

Well, it's a bit strange at first. Her potions and lotions clutter up the bathroom. Her pictures and postcards dot his plain walls. She has fanciful habits: hangs her colourful clothes over doors, lintels, picture-hooks. 'Like living in a circus tent!' he says. She finds his grandparents' silver wedding service boxed away, and starts using it at all the meals, or places pieces in odd corners – his father's christening tankard, catching the light, with a bundle of cherry twigs in it. 'Gannin' micey, lass?' he says, shaking his head. 'What's that?' she says, and he can't help laughing, that she's even forgotten the way they speak, here – if she ever knew.

She takes baths for hours, so he has to hammer on the door and bellow until she appears, wrapped in a towel, blinking water away in surprise. She goes on long, useless walks, and then orders clothes, and even food to the door, by post. Cheese! When they have plenty of food right here, and Rhonda Wood, on the neighbouring farm, is famous for her cheese. 'I can't ask her,' she says. 'I've never spoken to her.' This is such a pointless statement that he doesn't know what to say. This far from town, they don't need to speak to Rhonda and Farmer Wood. They know the Woods like they know the weather.

But overall, despite the constant presence of delivery vans, he is happier than he has ever been. This is love, he thinks. In the morning, he leaps out of bed to swill mouthwash around his gums and press a layer of wax into his hair before going back to kiss her awake. He cannot stop watching her, coming over to touch her; as she combs her glittering, red hair in the mirror, as she darts about the kitchen in one of her funny, dressing-gown dresses – he can't help reaching out to touch, to stroke – as she sits stroking the screen of her phone, or talking into it to her mother, as she does for hours. She closets herself in the sitting room for hours on end to make her phone calls: female things, he supposes. He loves to see the shape of her mouth, her little beating white throat. He wishes he could take that voice out to the fields for the long days. And turn over the sound of her in his tattered pocket, like a key or a trinket to bounce from palm to palm.

The only bother, at first, is that she's a prattler. A couple of times, she comes out to meet the tractor, and he waves, bouncing past, when he sees her leaning on the gate, mouthing his name. In the evening, he's weary to the bone when he comes in, and ready to collapse in front of the television after dinner. 'Shall we go to visit my mother?' she'll ask; or: 'Do you want to play cards?' – even answering the radio and TV: 'What do you think of that?' – and he can only shake his head. He's a practical man; a man of hands, not words. He's only roused to some energy when he presses his fingers on her white legs. 'Shhh,' he murmurs, cradling her in his arms like he would a pint of beer.

At last, that niggling worry – *what will happen to the farm after I'm gone?* – is gone. Even if they never have children, he's completed a proper history for the family name. Of his father, they say: 'He married Mary Metcalfe and had one son; was the first man to bring in combine harvesting, died and is buried at…' Now, after he, himself, is gone, they'll say: 'He married the widow Ramsey's beautiful daughter, and invested in cold storage facilities for the potatoes. Once or twice a year, they'd throw these huge parties… Aye, I always liked the old man.'

*

He is happy, and so nothing needs to change. Then one day, relatively early on, he comes in for lunch to find the kitchen empty, the table and chairs turned neatly upside down on the lino. He thinks it must be one of her oddities, takes bread and that crumbly cheese from the fridge, leaves, stuffing them in his mouth as he walks back to the tractor. When he returns at five, the scene is the same, although the shadows are lengthening.

'Where are you?' he asks, loudly. She shouts something from the bedroom.

His mother wouldn't have had him shouting from room to room. Wouldn't've had him ready to eat the oven door on a night, neither. He thuds along the corridor and finds her lying on her back in bed in her nightdress, holding a small, leatherbound book and cupping her belly, watching the sunset. 'Why's house so dark?' he asks again, politely.

'I need to be asked, if you want me to do something,' she says. Her eyes are directed somewhere out of the window. His gaze follows, and he stamps over to look out. Is there something there?

But there is nothing there. He is confused. He has done exactly nothing to bring this upon himself. It's not fair, Mammy? 'I can't read your mind,' she says, lolling on the bed in her fleecy blanket, those big green eyes flicking away.

An irritation begins to scratch at him. 'Now, I don't want you shouting at me from the bedroom,' he says, and shakes his finger. 'Come and talk to me properly, if you want owt.'

'Talk! Talk, you say!' she says in sudden fury, rearing up from the padded headboard. His mother's headboard. 'You never talk! I've asked you when we're going to town! Are you trapping me here? You ate my cheese, though you said you didn't like it! You lied!'

This is just too foolish for him to respond to. Where has this come from?

He walks out of the bedroom and over to his parents, where, over a proper tea, his dad advises him women speak a different language to men, one that can't be understood with logic, as his mother silently spoons out second helpings of beef lasagne. Outside, the lasagne's sisters cavort in the paddock.

'Get her something,' his mother says, finally, passing round the box of treacle toffee at the end of the meal. 'Show her.'

He looks at her. She looks back, accusingly: grey eyes like pebbles and jaw working away at the toffee. 'Ga'arn,' is all she can say, drool collecting at the corner of her mouth.

'Like what?' he mumbles.

He watches her cheek bulge in, out. At last: 'I know you,' she says, a little indistinctly. 'You're soft as this claggum, but she won't know that. No need to fuss about it. Bring her something. To,' And she pauses. 'To show her what you mean.'

For a second, her teeth seem to be stuck together again, as she struggles to get something out.

'Bring her something, to – to be kind.'

*

He doesn't know what to get her from the shops, and she won't want a living or dead thing from the farm. 'Let's go for a drive,' he says to her, one morning. She turns and gapes at him. Even her teeth are pretty and little, he thinks. Of course, not long till they start clacking. 'Are we going to town? Where to? What for?' but he won't tell her. In the car, she quietens down once they take the turning that leads away from town. She slumps, just staring out of the dusty window at fields of spring rape until they arrive at the kennels.

He's especially in need, but he walks quickly down the aisle of cages checking for any collie bitches. Even an abandoned lurcher or beagle might be handy with the rabbits and the hares… But she's stopped, caught by something behind him. 'What's that?' he asks, half-turning, and she points at the mesh, unable to speak.

A cocker spaniel has just whelped. A Christmas gift that lasted till May, till it got thick in the belly and unpretty. The pups are rollocking and laiking all over each other in a squirming puddle of golden curls; reminding him, somewhat uneasily, of the lavishly brunette June on a Sports Direct calendar he used to have.

'Oh,' she says, and her eyes fill with tears as she reaches to pick up one wriggling cub in her arms. 'A baby. A little, tiny, baby.'

'We can get a cot for the baby,' he says, and she gives a sarcastic snort, still cuddling the beast. 'I'll paint the scullery in duck-egg and knit some hats,' she says, and he nods seriously. Her green eyes flick sideways to look at him in slight surprise. He nods again, like a puppet – he wants to show her he takes her seriously – and, slowly, the corners of her mouth start to lift.

'Whisht,' his Da would say. 'Farm dogs don't live inside.' Well, he doesn't need to tell her that yet. They seem to be in perfect understanding of each other again. He'll hold his tongue, he thinks: just for now.

That evening, the puppy sits in her lap as they watch TV, and peace reigns. At one point, she turns to him, mouth in an 'O' as if to speak – but then shuts it again, and gives him a pained smile. He dares to smile back. They watch to the end in complete silence. He is happier than he's ever been, he says to himself, astonished.

*

She is jolted awake.

The curtains are a block of grey against the dark of the room. It is very early: that time when it is still dark, but the sky is lighter than the earth– just. Early morning, then; and something is making a very small noise from the floor.

It is the kind of sound that translates clearly as need. She keeps her eyes tight shut while he, next to her, starts groaning, rolls around, then gets up: heavily and bringing the duvet up with him. The puppy, which she had put on the floor last night, now starts making a noise like boiling water. As the woman digs herself back into hibernation, she hears the man hiss in pain and tell the puppy to do something to itself before thumping out of the room. The puppy sniffs, as though in disdain at such unceremonious treatment, before beginning to totter around the bedroom, sniffing around at each corner and secret.

He will soon find that this house is taut as a leash. Silence lies thick on the floor and packed into the corners, the air stuffed with all that is unspoken. She and the man skirt around each other in polite denial, exchanging only the occasional glancing phrase. Their words bounce harmlessly off and away, as though she and he are encased in rubber. Even the puppy looks embarrassed to cause a disturbance, when he is caught pissing and chewing the chair legs. 'It's all right, baby!' she'll say, trying to reassure him – and herself – that it is normal to hear more than the wind and your own breath in your ears.

Sometimes, she looks at the puppy and wonders: can he sense the swirling undercurrent of tension, beneath? She herself can almost taste the streaky whiffs of Nivea cream, flaky eczema and old leather in the air, from the old farmhands who used to live here. It must be dull for him, she thinks, as she stands by the mounting pile of washing-up, watching him track a bluebottle across the kitchen. Apart from the occasional visit from the postman and Wood, there are only two humans living here: the man that plucked him from his mother's brindled side, and she herself, the one he belongs to, the female.

To a dog, their behaviour must be baffling. How illogical she must seem. She is a constant locker of doors: always shutting Puppy out of a room, or in; flying out in alarm if she hears the man's footsteps. When in the kitchen, she shows anger towards inanimate objects: clatters pans, slams cutlery on the table. She spends hours cooking elaborate, meatless meals and then chucks in fried sausages at the last minute, which the man and the dog gobble up first. She herself eats straight from the fridge, standing in its pool of cold light in the small hours. And after every phone call in her locked room, she shakes, snorts, leaks water from her eyes – after every phone call, regular as clockwork; whether it's the angry, deep voice she's speaking to, or the older, soothing female. Even the puppy, she thinks, who doesn't think in words exactly, even he – even through a door – must be able to tell that the male voice speaks from another land.

The woman sighs, standing over the sink, and leans sideways to press her forehead against the damp wall. A dog must be able to tell that the grammar and rhythm of this man's sentences move differently, she thinks. That they slide over each other in different hills and valleys – the threat of a volcano, here and there. For the disembodied man-voice at the end of the phone line, all objects dance around in genders: a girl-table, a woman-mountain. As opposed to their own flatly neutral wooden items in this place; this rolling world of foggy grey and green.

The calls usually end when the male voice erupts in a furious stream of begging. *S'il te plait, s'il te plait.* Then, the puppy listening at the door will only hear a *click*; and then she comes out of the sitting room, dabbing her eyes and smiling brightly.

She weeps, too, each time she gets her monthlies, and notices that at this time of the month, the puppy seems to get a little more excited. He dances under her feet when she enters a room. Able to smell, perhaps, the chemical prickle on her skin; sense the dark blood eddying. Or perhaps it's simply because he feels raised emotions in one of his pack? Hears her start sniffing and snorting again, when she pulls down her knickers and finds the red flag there again. She remembers with a mental shudder the chewed teats of his dam in the kennels when she rolled onto her back, trying to pull away from the litter. It must be baffling to him, why women do it. There must be some biological propulsion to self-propagate, tricking them.

Animals, she thinks, feeling her mouth twist bitterly as she stares at the washing-up. All we think about is breeding and eating. There's nothing more to us than that. Why do we even have language, when it ties you up in knots in these ways? Why bother with thoughts? We would be happier without.

*

And if the dog doesn't understand her, nor does the man. His eyes follow the woman's every movement, longingly; his brows wrinkled upwards with yearning in much the same way that the puppy looks at mince. The man is utterly blind to what the woman sees when she peers in a mirror: the chipped front tooth, the fat blue veins on the backs of her legs (hairless as a sick whippet's), the bits of herself she pinches and sighs at. But the second she turns to look at the man, he'll drop his gaze onto his newspaper or tin of bean, pretending he wants nothing from her.

They are at breakfast. The puppy starts begging for another piece of sausage. He tilts his head and whines: he cannot say 'I want', but his whole body trembles to convey his yearning. The woman lets out a grudging giggle and gets up, to fetch the puppy a treat. 'Lovely boy,' she murmurs as she squats down to feed him. Bastard creature, the man thinks, watching out of the corner of his eye, and suddenly realises that his own head is slowly sliding into a pleading tilt, just like the dog's. He rights himself immediately. Shifts awkwardly in his chair.

They do not speak to each other. Somewhere along the way, the man feels, they made a bargain, and the house is straining to keep to it. But he can feel waves of resentment pouring off her like smoke, all the time – it almost makes him cough! He doesn't understand it: Why is she angry? Why doesn't she just tell him, if she's angry? The words clump in his throat like rocks every time he tries to bring it up, and he feels miserable. He does not know what to do but look, and touch; he is always trying to touch her, fiddling with her hair, giving her sharp shoulders a quick stroke as he walks past. At the end of each day, he says: 'Bed?' hopefully.

And she might fleetingly pass a hand on her stomach – so quickly that you'd barely notice, unless you are her dog – and nods.

Now, he watches sadly as the puppy grins and puts his paw on her knee to try to get her attention. She puts her skinny hand on top of the paw and looks down into engorged pupils. 'Oh, baby,' she says, and the man can see that, again, her eyes are watering. 'Oh, my baby.'

*

Obviously, things cannot go on like this. The air is stringy with ifs and maybes and perhapses. You walk through them strung across doorframes, brush your hand on their stickiness under the table. The puppy's nails click on the kitchen lino. Click-clack, click-clack: you can hear him snuffling and clickering, wherever you are in the house. The man rustles a page of his newspaper, abruptly irritated. 'Hush, dog, or you'll be outside.'

Things cannot go on like this. They need some kind of middleman, the man thinks. One lunchtime, daringly, he brings his father in with him from the field. They stand in the gloom of the corridor; two lanky, stooped men in torn coats, clumsily stamping mud off their boots. She, hearing heavy footsteps, comes barrelling out of her room in alarm and skids to a halt in front of them. 'Oh,' she says. 'Now then,' the man says. 'Now then,' the old man says, awkwardly. There is a long silence.

'And why won't your wife come and talk to me?' she says suddenly, tugging her dressing-gown – crumpled peacock satin – closer around her. Her eyes are red-rimmed.

'Why, lass, she's wanting you to settle in, like,' says the old man, after a pause. Puppy, winding around the woman's calves, whines.

'She's wanting to silence me,' flares the woman, stepping forward. 'She's wanting me to grow tired and grow old before she'll see me – she's frightened of me!'

The old man's mouth thins. His eyes glaze over, and he turns and pushes past the man on his way outside.

The man pauses, raises a hand to his face, then drops it. He takes an uncertain step towards her. 'Don't be blathering skite,' he says at last, then turns and rushes after his father.

The woman stands there, then spins on her heel and goes back into her bedroom. The puppy follows, wagging his tail, and sits on his haunches as she starts rifling in her wardrobe, turning over silks and woollens until she pulls out something small and glittering; small enough to keep in her closed fist. She looks at the puppy, watching quietly from the floor, and laughs bitterly. 'I've made my choice,' she says to him. 'I need to accept it. I'm here, now. The end.' And then she sits down to make marks on paper.

The puppy observes for a few seconds, then wanders off to see if he can find any open cupboards in the kitchen. But he hasn't been sniffing around for long before she reappears, the pale lilac odour of hysteria drifting after her. She hunkers down awkwardly on the grimy lino and brandishes a small package of letters tied together with twine. 'This is the past,' she says, an underlying note of shrillness belying the calmness of her voice.

She stands up, scraping a chair back to sit. She pulls a cigarette lighter out of her pocket, and starts setting light to the letters, one by one. The puppy presses his long nose into flesh of her calf and looks up, the neurones in his small brain attracted by the brightly-coloured stamps, the stiff postcards. A volcano, bright green hills, neon sea, and on the other side, black words curling up and dissolving into velvet flakes.

'Once upon a time,' says the woman. 'The End.' Her lower lip wobbles and her eyes brim.

The puppy gives a soothing bark. Is this an invitation to her, to say more?

But then the man drifts in, ready for his lunch. 'Lunch?' he is murmuring hopefully; peering into all the pans untidily left out on the hob, and the woman gets up so fast that the man doesn't even notice she's sponging ashes away.

*

After burning the letters, the woman seems to age twenty years overnight. It is as she said: she has grown tired and therefore silent: the words have gone out of her. She slumps. Her arms and legs hang off her shoulders and hips like string, and she starts a habit of worrying at her frayed nails with her teeth.

It is the height of the summer, and the man is out from dawn till dusk working with his father and Neighbour Wood, but even he seems to notice, when he comes home stinking of sweat and dusty with hayseed. And yet, still, all he manages to mumble is, 'Had a good day, then? Good.'

And then, later: 'News?' and then: 'Bed?'

The puppy's nose moves in miniscule twitches as he moves, picking up the slightest quiver of an enzyme. His eyes are weaker, but even in grey shades, it's obvious to him: the white cradle of the telephone is twin to the open bowl of the fridge. She feeds from both – she lives off the words that the telephone sends and without them, she's starving to death. When the man comes in from another day, the puppy is waiting by the door. The man almost trips over him, kicking his own shin in an effort to twist out of the way before he catches himself and swears richly at the dog for the trouble.

He is sorry almost as soon as the curses have left his lips, of course; feels his cheeks redden and glances nervously behind him. Nobody is there, of course. Nobody has seen his embarrassing unbalancing or heard his uncouth words. He bites his tongue in penance – think of how Ma would scold – but the dog seems to pay no attention to his humiliation, only rising from where it lay to bark urgently at him. The man brushes grass off his shoulders and looks at the dog, alarmed. The puppy shakes his long, curling ears, raises its eyebrows, growls meaningfully, and slinks off.

The man blinks. For a second, he could have believed the dog was trying to tell him something.

He shakes his head. 'Eejit,' he mutters, and starts pulling off his boots.

However, it appears the man does take in something of what the puppy tells him, whatever it is. One morning, the woman is in the kitchen making something with sugar and eggs, both of which are vaguely disgusting to a dog. She hums sweetly, smacking eggs into a mixing bowl, and does not notice as his wagging behind rounds the corner and disappears out of the door.

Cocker spaniels are so named because they catch cocks; that is, roosters and woodcocks. Bulky, ground-nesting birds: ripe for the plucking. The puppy does not have a mother or siblings around him to teach him how to lurk and pounce. But it is easy to see blood instinct shivers through his body, from trembling nose. He wriggles catlike around the half-open door of the bedroom, and stops, triumphant. For, what's this? The man is here: sitting on the clean quilt, at midday, in his filthy, tattered waxed coat.

The puppy lets out a single, questioning bark. The man barely glances up, staring at something he holds obscured in one spadelike hand. 'Shh,' he says, exaggeratedly miming a finger on lips, as though the dog is some kind of idiot.

This puppy grins and lets his tongue hang out, demonstrating friendliness. As much as he's the woman's dog, it was the man who gave him to her. Besides, the man is built like a fallen oak, to someone of the puppy's size, and smells something like a bull.

The man is breathing heavily. 'I'm only doing this because I don't understand her, any more,' he says to the puppy, sadly. 'She doesn't speak to me as she used to.' He looks to the puppy, as if expecting a reply. The puppy only looks back, grinning. 'As if she ever did, you turkey,' mutters the man.

He turns back to the little book and starts turning the pages. He reads slowly at first, and as he does, the central fold on his forehead deepens. A neat furrow, ploughed down his face. As he makes his way through, he flicks gradually faster, and faster, growing more and more impatient, as if looking for something, but with no idea what – until, at last, he lets out a frustrated snort and tosses the diary on the floor.

The pages aren't covered in left-to-right sentences; just lists, disjointed scraps of words and phrases. The dog trots over and gives it a nudge with his nose, catching the sense of secrets. He slurps his tongue out, turning a few pages to the last one she has written on: the last the man saw.

Here. Shapes:

Pack everything	*brazil nuts*
Polish	*feta*
Lay fire	*organic raisins*
Strip bed	*dark chocolate*

The man watches, bitterly. These words mean about as much to him as they do to the puppy, who has already grown bored and given up on the book. He turns and whines at the door, as the man leans forward and picks the book up again.

'Does she mean to escape, eh?' mutters the man, turning the pages and staring at the paper again. 'With someone Polish…?'

The puppy's tail is thumping on the floor steadily. 'You're right, I am a clod,' says the man, sighing again. He reaches out a hand to pat Puppy, just as she steps sideways to frame herself in the doorway.

'There're no secrets there,' she says.

'Jesus! – '

'None that you couldn't simply have asked for, anyway.'

There is a pause.

'Are you running away?' says the man, and – he just can't help himself – he scratches his head.

Silent as a mushroom, thinks the woman; a parasite that sprouts on saplings. A gingery night-fungus of a man.

Aloud, she says: 'This house is a mausoleum,' and takes a deep breath. She's made every effort, she tells him, but he was bound to carrying on the past, and there's no cure for that.

The midday sun is spilled over the bed and lights her up as she steps into the room. She tilts her head and smiles, but her voice is cold as the blade of a knife and bears no hint of humour.

She's always been a practical woman, she says.

This rouses him. 'That's not true,' he says, nervously. 'You're sat about the house all the day, wearing silks and satins.'

'I cook!' she says, in instant rage. 'I clean! I've tried to make the best of this house. I wear my mother's old clothes!'

What they both say is true. They glower at each other in silence.

She's practical, she says, at last. She'd had to be, when she was travelling all over the world – you can't be a woman that cares about fashions and ironing, when you're moving around all the time – but she longed for a family. For comfort, and for friendships that lasted years, not weeks – for community, for people.

'Why, you could've befriended the Woods, if you hadn't dithered,' he tries.

She talks over him as though he has said nothing. She'd always had some idea in her head of a soft, green land, she says.

Somewhere back where her mother was, she says, where she herself could have a child. And when her last job had come to an end, on the island, and it became clear that her lover was not going to bring her such settled comfort as her mother and mother-land, she'd decided that, this time, she'd break her own heart. She'd bring that story to a close, on purpose, to force herself into a new beginning. Again: once upon a time.

The man is gaping blankly at her.

So she came back, she says, her voice rising. To her mother, and this snotrag of a country. Green and grey and always damp and trailed with mist, this mucous land. She tried to be a woman again. She couldn't bear pink, or the tight, glitzy clothes other women wore, so she put on her mother's tattered old dressing-gowns and felt more like herself. And when her nitwit cousin had suggested she try out a date, she'd been persuaded, hadn't she.

And the manchild had a bumfluffy beard and spots and a stammer, but he'd seemed honest, at least, unlike the last one. She'd had enough of men who spoke two languages: a half-man who hiccuped his words seemed enough for her.

He feels anger slowly piling up inside him, word by word, but there is no latch to let it out, and her words seem to tumble out so easily in contrast, rushing at him in an unstoppable flood, washing his helpless arguments away.

She thought: if they understood each other, why not? she says. She told her cousin to make the deal plain. No romance, no ideals: he should be grateful, and she'd get a home and a family and adoration for it. 'Why else,' she said now (her brows twisting) 'would a woman like me move in with a man like you?'

And she'd tried to keep her side of the bargain. But he hadn't told her what she'd promised to. He'd locked her up like some princess in a fairy tale.

His silence loomed, she says. Does he realise how loud silence is, from a tall man? He'd wrap his arms around her in a bearhug, saying *Shhh-shh*. He laid a threatening hand on her – a hand like a trowel. God, he wouldn't stop touching her. Pinching her. With his fingers like sausages – she is so sick of sausages, God!

'Do you realise how loud it is, silence?' she asks, bitterly. When he *Shh-shh*'d her, she'd clam up. Women learn these things young. She'd had a mad ex-boyfriend, once: women learn how to smile, how not to speak, when spoken to. Or else they don't get very far.

But gradually, she says, she'd realised that in spite of the earth in his beard and the dirt under his fingernails, he was as dreamy as a teenage girl. He gave her gifts in place of words – well, she believes he'd sooner she was gathering dust on a bookshelf, like his mother's silver, and was taken down only to handle at bedtime. Does he live in the past? Or was it the future, as he was always only thinking of how they'd be remembered when they were rotting in the ground? Wherever it was, it was in some alternate reality to the one they were in.

She, feeling exultant anger, looks at the man on the bed to see how he's going to answer her. He is not looking up. He looks half the size: crumpled like a piece of tarpaulin. She feels a momentary twinge of guilt; but dismisses it.

She's a real woman, she says to him, in that same hard tone. She's no fairytale. He'd some idea in his head, she says. And he had tried his damnedest to silence her words, and he damned well nearly did it. Through silence, that was all.

'Instead of speaking to me,' she says, 'You gave me a dumb animal.'

She laughs. Even to her ears, it sounds shocked.

'You'll not see your mother again,' she says. He half-lifts his head.

'I will,' he says; but his voice sounds like a chair with a wobbling leg.

'You'll not,' she says, with satisfaction. Her eyes move to the puppy, who hasn't made a noise through all of this, and her eyes soften. 'You can go, baby,' she says to the puppy. 'We can speak to each other, now. We don't need you, any more.'

*

And so things change. It is not all her way; they compromise. The man and the woman drive away together one day, and return with a neat pinewood kennel for the puppy, outside. They do not need something to speak between them, any more. Sometimes, the man will be in the lighted kitchen in the evening, listening to her voice unfurling in a story, and will jump, look out of the window, on hearing a twin howl spiralling up into the night.

The mother comes to call, of course, after a few weeks of her boy not seeing her. She marching towards them from across the fields: a moving, distant dot, getting closer and closer. When she arrives, she swings a leg over the fence and walks to stand, hand-hipped, in front of the kitchen window, looking like an iron rake.

The woman opens the window and leans out: they stare at each other. Old face to young face, hinny to mare.

'How'd you get here?' asks the woman.

'Shanks' pony,' replies the other.

The woman laughs, a bright carolling sound. 'Why don't you speak a language anyone can understand?' she says. She does not wait for an answer, pulling herself back inside and slamming the window, and the mother turns and tramps away, back over the fields. Nothing more needs saying.

The man is in the living room, painting its insides with magnolia. He watches the whole thing, seeing his mother stride away, then looks at the dog and wonders if he's imagining its look of sympathy. Dogs cannot talk.

When she enters the room, supporting her belly that goes before her, he does not know what to say. 'Why didn't you say something to her?' he asks, at last.

A smile curves her mouth. 'I was as loud as I could be,' she says.

Cull Yaw

I.

Bleed it. Skin it. Hang it. Cut it. That is how you make food from an animal. Chefs lie about this, in the words they use: they call the bled, skinned sheep 'mutton', or the baby cow 'veal'. Butchers and cooks hit the animal even when it's dead. They bash steak with a rolling-pin. Hammer the veal escalope. Pin a duck's wings to its sides and put it in an instrument called a duck press – that is, an intstrument of suffocation, to kill without making a cut, so that the blood can be retained for a sauce. They call it: 'tenderizing'.

This is one of the reasons why I do not eat meat: it is a lie. He used to use soft words. Andouillette, he'd say to me. Carpaccio, tartare – just try it! The onions sizzle on your tongue…

Thin strips of skin! I would reply. Peppered flesh of pig! Think about where it comes from. No, really. Think about it. That's what you don't want to think about, isn't it? The blood and the guts. Muck on skin. Big, shiny eyes, looking at you.

He'd laugh, and shy away like a horse. Before we met, I didn't understand how people could eat meat, let alone how I could ever be with someone who ate meat. Kiss them, press my lips on theirs and run my tongue around their mouth. I don't know if it's a good thing, the way we can hold two things in our heads at the same time.

Bleed it, skin it, hang it, he says, now. His voice is shaking. The thing is lying on the table in front of us.

It'll be easy, I say, trying to sound soothing. We'll just tell him it's in the middle of ageing, and that's why it looks a bit different to the usual cut. He'll never know.

I can hear my own steady voice, but I can feel my heart in my mouth and it's pulsing with terror, because I can see him turning a pale yellowy colour, and for a second I think he is never going to go through with it.

Easy, now, I say, and to my relief, he swallows. Blinks a few times, takes a breath and turns towards it.

I let out a slow whistle of breath that I didn't know I was holding. He has to do this. We have to. I have to. It's me that is giving up the most, here. But I have to, because otherwise I would be giving up in a different way, and I won't. I don't want to give up, give him up, and go back. And certainly, after doing this, there is no going back to anything.

*

We connected on an app when I moved back here, though actually we'd known each other since school. We'd both gone to the local comp, had friends in common. We'd never really spoken, but I'd always kept half an eye on him: dark and pretty-looking through the window of the butcher's on Saturdays. I'd wait outside for my mother, trying to catch a peek at his arms. Even then, trying to avoid seeing flashes of the raw meat that he expertly flipped and skewered, the dirty-white bones. Later, when I was at college, I'd see him sometimes by the bins outside The Fox & Hounds, shivering in his chef's whites and puffing on a vape. Later still, when I washed up back here again, I heard vaguely that he'd taken over his dead dad's farm, was involved in some kind of legal dispute with his brother, was doing mad, modern things: rewilding and investing in ethical meat production, even building his own, small farm shop for wholesale.

Organic, you know, my mother said, when we were in her kitchen one day. Supplies food to all the posh restaurants in Leeds and Harrogate – and Sheffield, too! Just fancy, you've might've been to one of them, when you were in Sheffield. Eaten food he's grown, in a fancy restaurant. From right *here*!

I stared absently at the split ends of her long, yellowish hair, and thought of the watery porridge I gulped on grey Sheffield mornings, sitting on my mattress. The cold potatoes I used to carry in my pocket for my lunch break at work, before the environmental centre had made cuts and I'd been fired.

My mother's eyes were fixed hungrily on me. I kept my gaze on a point located somewhere around her elbows. Such a nice boy! she said. You know, it's getting downright *Guardian*-reading round here, Star. The farmers are getting downright middle-class!

My mother looked like a damp and broken umbrella. She flung out one arm in a wild and apparently pointless gesture, presumably because she thought it was the sort of dramatic arm movement people made when discussing the class system. Her mildewed black sleeve trailed through a spill of oats on the kitchen counter.

Well, times are a-changing, round here! she said, gleefully. Nasty, dirty lot they used to be, when we first came here, Star. You won't remember, no, you were only tiny, but unwelcoming, to a poor single mother. A backwards lot. Dirty, scum. Yes, times are a-changing, and I, for one, am all for it. It's all your kind of stuff, Star, isn't it, this stuff? The organic? Well, I used to do all that stuff too, once upon a time...

Her voice dropped and rose, from wheedling to vicious and back again.

Well, I'm only an old woman, now. Look to the young people, that's what I've always said. Us old guys, we should be learning from you.

I counted fence posts through the grimy window behind her. She'd never got around to putting curtains up, though she'd lived here over twenty years. *I'm not that kind of bourgeois mummy-housewife, Star!* Then she'd whine about none of the neighbours liking her. *Bitches, nasty. A lower-class lot.*

She had to stop and cough, panting for breath. I could see every bone in her chest, even through that ridiculous black gauzy thing.

You know that rapeseed oil I've got? she said, as soon as she'd gathered herself. The one with the picture of the little blonde girl on it? It's from a farm just a few miles from Thirby Moor, they've di-ver-see-fied.

She tapped out each syllable with her tongue, leaning forward. Read about him in the *Yorkshire Post* magazine, she said. He looked such a nice young man. All of these nice young men, Star, eh! That's a change, too, from old times, I'll tell you. They had pictures of him with his family. All blonde. The little girl's on the bottle. Look, I'll get it.

Don't bother, I said, but she was already struggling through coughs to reach into the cupboard, holding a twiggy arm across her mouth and making disgusting hacking noises. The cupboard was empty, except for a few cans of her Weightwatchers minestrone, baggies of weed 'for my joints'; and, now, a glass bottle with twine wrapped around it.

Got to support local businesses! she said, turning to me gleefully and wiping her mouth. She shoved the oil at me. I must say, she said. It's nice that it's changing, round here. Gentrification's not just something for you townies, any more!

Round here's not exactly gentrified, I said. That's why I had to come back, isn't it, because here's the only place I could afford. I think that rapeseed farmer is an ex-hedge fund manager.

She turned around jerkily, and bumped her elbow on the microwave. Ow, she cried, and started coughing again, long hair falling over her face. When she stopped, and pushed it back, her eyes were watering even more.

Oh, you, she said, and jabbed a shaking finger at me, clearly unable to speak for rage. You think I'm old and stupid, don't you, she said in a trembling voice. Well, you'll see. We can't all afford to have principles like you, princess. You'll have to work in McDonalds. You'll have to get a proper. Blooming. Job, and work hard, for once in your life, like the rest of us who got cornered by life. Who get *trapped*. You'll give up. You'll see.

We glared balefully at each other, in silence. At last, I told her I was going out, and left.

Since I'd been forced to move back in, I'd been avoiding the few of my old friends who still lived here. Salma, Sam, Sophie. I'd taken to catching the bus out to the edge of the estate, going on long walks across bare ploughed fields. Doing something so useless was a way of pretending that all that was the matter with me was being here. But, if I was honest, I'd felt useless for a long time. At the environmental centre, when they were letting me go, they'd said they felt like there was something passive about me. Greg and Jane, the bosses with money draining out of their pockets, sitting there with smug, sad expressions. *We never felt enough from you, Star. We just don't know if you care.*

The pub was still open as I passed, and a couple of men were lolling about outside. Pale men, like uncooked sausages. Oi, s'that old hippie's kid, back again! one said. They all started belching laughter and I hurried to flag down the bus, trying not to breathe in their smoke, their barbequed-meat smell. Stumbled into a seat and started scrolling.

So, pretty butcher boy is single, I thought, and swiped right without imagining that he'd ever notice, or reply.

*

hi, he wrote. hi, I wrote back. i know you right? he wrote. sophie's neighbour, I wrote. i just moved back here. of course, he wrote. i remember you. fancy a pint then?

It was a lazy golden evening. I walked up to the roundabout at the top of the estate, walked past the pub. Only one man was hanging around, small and balding like a sacked cherub, tugging on a cigarette so small he looked like he was biting his thumb. He stared at me as I walked past.

I walked on. Walked to where the houses ended. Pushed through the trees at the back of the estate, followed the trodden path down to the clearing where older kids had always gone to smoke and make out. Midges swirled above the beck, someone's beer cans floated in the amber water below his dangling feet.

We sat on a patch of scraped earth and talked. Haltingly, at first: our conversation strung with silences like beads on a necklace. We spoke of old friends, old teachers, the new supermarket, while listening hard to the white spaces in between words: the gaps, the pauses spotting our conversation like lacework. He told me about dropping out of catering college and the Young Farmers; I told him about Crookes, anarchists and raves. Neither of us mentioned the obvious: what we put in our mouths.

I had not been so near another person for a long time. The hairs rose up on my arms whenever he shifted position; I'd forgotten I was an animal, too. *You don't really care*, hissed Greg and Jane inside my head, and I tried to remind myself that I was just here to distract myself for a few hours; that he was a farmer, a killer; that my prickling skin was bristled just like a pig's when its dead body was spun in the dehairing machine. But I could not see the pig, somehow. His hulking body blocked it out: heat rising from it and filling the air with Lynx and beating with blood and flesh, and the sensation was too much: I felt queasily unable to move. When I closed my eyes, I could still see the midges swirling in points of golden light.

We separated at the bus stop, and I stopped to watch him go. He walked quickly, square hands stuffed like rocks into his pockets. My heart was still thudding, my head still felt light and in shock. I was thinking that I'd fucked it, that he must've thought I was a bloodless, pale skin of a girl. I had felt bloodless, until now.

A scraped voice came from behind me. You know, that lad doesn't have many friends round here, it said, and I turned, and found myself facing the grimy little cherub, puffing on his fag-end, eyes narrowed at me.

*

For our second date, he asked me to meet him at the farm shop. He came out from behind the freezer, massive in a white polystyrene apron and wiping his fingers. When he leaned in to kiss me on the cheek, I smelled a waft of something sweet, cold, red and yet warm; and had to hold myself rigid not to pull away.

When I managed to meet his eyes, he was frowning uncertainly, evidently sensing something. How about some fresh air? he said. Rebecca can watch the shop. That OK, Bex?

Rebecca had long, blonde hair and was wearing one of those Indian block-printed dress. Um, yah, she said, looking daggers at me, and we went outside, into the sun.

A field of young barley looks like water, moves like silver. We stood in the scruffy car park and stared out at the land flowing beyond. He planted his hands on his hips and stared out. Have you ever eaten meat, then? he asked.

Never, I said. Couldn't bear it, and he nodded, seriously.

I care about my animals, you know, he said.

You kill them, I wanted to say. Instead, I let my eyes slide to the small, scooped hollow at the base of his sunburnt neck. My mouth was dry.

I get it, he said. But I dunno how I could live here, without farming. How I'd make a living. Or the lads that work at the farm, what'd they do if I didn't pay them? I've thought about selling the farm, but then the sheep'd go to some farmer that wouldn't worry about keeping them happy, I guess, and everyone'd be worse off.

Yeah, I said.

I've killed my animals myself, he said, looking at me with those bright eyes. I learnt how. Be deceiving myself if I hadn't. I care about them.

His eyes skipped down over the curve of my breasts, and he looked away quickly. I didn't know what it was about this man that had overwhelmed me: his flat, half-open words, his gentleness and deft hands; and, underneath, the sweetish scent of dead blood, the trembling nervous systems of living things that he'd dug his fingernails into. I couldn't untangle it all: this man who was making me shake with wanting to run my hands down his chest, and shiver with wanting to pull back, wipe him off my palms.

He stood feet apart and whistled. I shaded my eyes. All I could see ahead of me was the flat shimmer of barley, the sun beating down from a headache-blue sky. Something was shivering among the stalks, moving towards us. He called something, a single, sharp syllable, and she came limping out, her tail wagging.

Good girl, Meg, he said, squatting and flinging out his arms, and she shambled over. An old coat come alive. A great big, mangy, black sheepdog flecked with gold and grey. This is Star, Meggie, he said.

Her dignity, next to the stupid name my mother gave me.

She looked up, grinning, pink tongue hanging out of her mouth, and obligingly trotted over. Hiya, I said, and crouched to help her as she attempted to scramble up my legs. He was laughing happily, and I snatched a look at him as Meg lurched up in my arms trying to lick my face, to see him silhouetted against the sun.

*

For our third date, I came to his farm. This time, I was resolved to put a stop to it, whatever *it* was. My stomach rose up whenever he came into my mind; I could not eat. Was this what people meant, when they said they felt sick with it?

He stood at the stove and I sat at the kitchen table, his huge back rising in front of me. I'd noticed the way Rebecca at the farm shop watched him, a piece at a time. His shoulders flexing. The chunks of his calves. The dark purpling tendons in his neck when he grappled with a sack.

'S a chocolate mole. Mexican. he said. Heat. Chocolate. Supposed to be an aphrodisiac, isn't it. He ducked his head, and grinned bashfully before turning back to the stovetop. Ancho chillies like dried brown fingers, simmered in a saucepan of water then scooped out. He tilted the pan to show me. Infuses the water with heat, he said. Got to be careful not to touch my eyes.

I felt the sting in the air, scratching my throat. He was talking in starts as he cooked. Telling me about the farm he'd inherited on the old man's sudden death. It was sad, obviously. But, in some ways, it made things easier, he thought. He'd seen what happened, when sons grew up and started arguing with their dads over how to run the farm. Useless old farts never knew when to stop and step aside for a new idea.

Prince Charles, I said, and he looked up and laughed suddenly. Yeah, I'm him, he said, his eyes resting on me appreciatively. I felt my shoulders relax backwards a little. He turned back to the stove and went on, more animatedly. Like, he, himself, was really into ethical farming. But his dad'd never liked him talking about that, so he'd basically had to bugger off, hadn't he? Left his little brother to deal with the old sod. And then, when his dad died... Well, he'd come back and tried again. Sustainability was the future, wasn't it. And now, his little brother was arguing that this wasn't what their dad would've wished, and it was running the farm into the ground; was taking him to court. But it would work. He'd show all that backwards lot round here...

Yeah, I said. Backwards lot. That made me think of my mother. What was she up to, alone in the house? Rattling around coughing, wiping her wet nose with toilet roll and tearing up squares of newspaper to use for the actual toilet. *I thought you liked recycling!* she'd squeal. When she bought everything wrapped in clingfilm, anyway. *Well, so I made a mistake*, she'd say, her chin wobbling. *I'm just an old woman, I'm trying to be more like you, pet, darling Star...* Why did she have to dig her claws into everything, even my thoughts?

Cull yaw, he said.

What? I said.

I'm trying to change this farm, he said. Trying to do it in the best way I can. I'm same as you, I really am.

His dad sold baby lambs to supermarkets, he explained, but what he himself really wanted to do was look for businesses that would buy meat from older animals. Cull yaw, the farmers called it: old ewe, basically. You slaughtered it once it'd had a good, long life, then aged the meat like Ibérico.

Like – you what? I said.

Ibérico ham! he said, and laughed, shaking his head at me. Salted, savoury, strong. So dry, you can shave curls off it with a razor. It gets blackened, it's so old, and the fat tastes like cream on the turn. This thick.

He measured an inch in the air with his finger. The supermarkets, and most farmers, thought the older meat was disgusting, he told me. But why were we so afraid of age? Old animals should be made use of. It meant getting off the capitalist wheel of breed-shear-fatten-slaughter – which was much crueller, and more wasteful, and conned the farmers and farmhands as well as the animals.

He moved swiftly and smoothly as he talked, one arm reaching up for the grater hanging from its peg at the same time as the other opened a drawer. Death and age is part of life, he said. Supermarkets, they put carcasses on ice, wrap 'em in plastic and pump them with enzymes. Take all the flavour out. Take out the tripe, the lungs, everything that pumps and pulses and stinks, so people can pretend they're eating, fucking, beef perfume instead of a living thing. It's not right.

Death and age is part of life. His words sent a wave of revulsion lurching through me – *wrong, you're wrong* – and yet at the same time I could not tear my eyes off him. I remembered watching him covertly from outside the butcher's shop as a teenager. Glimpses of his hands, in latex gloves smeared with grease and blood: the same fingers I secretly wanted to suck, the hands I wanted squeezing my thighs. Now, it was the way the veins in his wrist bulged as he squeezed a lime, the pepper of his sweat in the air. He was just the first man I'd happened across, up in this godforsaken dead-end place, I tried to tell myself. That was all. A nauseous mixture of guilt and desire rolled in my stomach.

He was staking everything on all this, he said cheerfully, as he stirred the mole. He'd cancelled the contract his dad'd had with Tesco, and he was meeting with a new distributor soon. One that supplied ethical produce. When he'd trained as a chef, he'd eaten at some of the restaurants that these particular distributors supplied to, and that was what decided him, when his dad died, on getting back to farming. Course, his brother wasn't pleased. But when you've tried seared eight-year-old leg of lamb with its own bone marrow, smoked, in a tart on the side, you can't go back to using PVC-wrapped, tortured pap –

A pause. Sorry, he said. I shouldn't've said –

No, don't worry –

I didn't mean. Does it gross you out?

No, honest. It's what I have to talk about too, at work.

Cool. Well. Sorry –

You can talk about your job. Honest.

Well. If you're sure it dun't upset you. Stop me if I talk about dry-aged meat too much. He grinned, shrugged. Johnno and Foster, the lads who work on the farm with me, are sick of hearing me bang on, and they're not even vegetarian.

I think animals deserve old age, I said, feeling myself go red. Not like some people.

We laughed stiffly, and then there was a brief silence. I watched him slice and chop vegetables for the mole. Chop and slice, his fingers like a gobbling mouth chewing, spitting out, regurgitating bite-sized chunks of squash and shallot, white potato and dark chocolate. The veins rising out of his forearm. I thought: this man could hurt me.

He wiped his hands on his apron and started to untie it, turning to smile at me. I've never made this vegetarian, before, he said. But I think it'll go even better with these new potatoes than with chicken.

I realised I could not leave. My elbows resting on the green oilcloth on the table. Candlelight, the air itself felt like warm water lapping at my skin. I could taste its salt and spice on my tongue. I felt my mouth curving back into a smile, thought: yes, this man could really hurt me.

*

I woke in his rumpled sheets early the next morning. My face felt sore, from being rubbed against his stubble. I licked my lips: salt.

He was a white slab rolled up in a duvet, snoring. I looked at him and wanted to touch. I wanted his tongue sliding down me, wanted my mouth open and his fingers in it. But instead I slid out of bed trying not to make a sound, pulled on my clothes, and scuttled downstairs. I let myself out of the front door and took a quick breath of cold air, then started walking back to my mother's house. The dead end.

*

The road was like a sloughed skin, edged with silvery trails of crisp packets and Irn-Bru cans. I paused at a gate to see if I could spot any of his old ewes in the field: the ones he'd blessed with an old age. I imagined what my former colleagues would've said, horrified. *They're still dying, Star. He's literally wearing them out through forced breeding, then waiting till their exhausted bodies wear out before killing them. Think about it!*

The sheep were huddled in the corner of the field, under a young elm over at the other end of the fields. At my old job, I'd run a campaign to stop local councils cutting down ancient trees: ashes and elms of the type that had grown here since the last Ice Age. But diseases got most of these trees anyway. Dutch elm disease and ash dieback wait until a tree is mature before they pounce, so this particular young elm was just waiting until the fungus got to it. Another one that wouldn't have to go through the humiliations of a useless old age.

I peered at the sheep and they peered back at me with their eerie yellow eyes. They had horizontal pupils, like aliens. You OK? I said to one of them. The sheep chewed stolidly, then rumbled something deep in its gullet, and I felt a familiar, frustrated lump rise in my throat at its stubborn stillness. Its total refusal to engage with me. There was something I recognised, in the animals round here. This sheep was powerless, sliding downhill towards death in a back-of-beyond land. What could it do about anything that happened to it? Nothing. So why should it bother reacting to me? Greg and Jane didn't understand that passivity could be a choice. They didn't see how, in this kind of place, silence could be a cold, hopeless anger, too.

Of course, it was stupid to project my own soppy crap onto animals. I looked at the sheep, blankly chewing its cud and ignoring me, and wished people would just leave these animals in peace, without either hurting them or sentimentalising them.

At least he was honest about it. At least he knew what death was.

Walking up the pebbledashed path and about to slot my keys into the lock, I realised the front door was ajar. It hung like lips slightly parted, an intake of breath. Mam? I said foolishly, standing there holding my key like a tiny gun. I pushed and stepped in. Inside, all was dark. Star, I heard my mother say in her gravelly voice, from somewhere low down. Star, Star.

Where's the light! I said, thumping my palms across the wall, and banged straight into a shelf.

Oh, whined my mother on the ground. Don't be angry, pet. I'm sorry.

S'not your fucking fault! I said, scrabbling along the wall and finding only damp plasterboard. Where are you? Where fucking are you?

She was a pile at the bottom of the stairs: the umbrella, broken. To my surprise, she wasn't crying, unlike her usual leaking self. Her eyes rested blankly on me.

Where's it hurt? I asked.

M'hips, she grated. M'ankle. My old bones. Oh, silly me, silly me. Help me up, my Star. I'm so glad you're here, pet. I'm so glad you came back.

I called an ambulance. I tried to explain to her that it was best if I didn't move her and didn't help her up. I stayed at a distance. I brought her a cup of tea and tilted it carefully on her lips so I didn't accidentally touch her cheek – bruised like a soft apple – with my hand. I had to look away to keep myself from slapping her when she dribbled milky tea out of the corners of her mouth. Pathetic. When the paramedics came, they said it was lucky I was there.

I'm only here temporarily, I told them. I don't live here, not since I was a kid.

The paramedic gave me a shrewd look. Well, he said. It looks like a significant fall, I can tell you that. Good thing you're here now.

Star, I heard my mother droning from the stretcher, like a machine stuck on repeat. Star, Star, Star.

*

Oh, said Salma, when I told her about my mother's fall. Have you visited hospital?

I told her I hadn't.

Oh. How come?

I told her my mother and I had a difficult relationship, and besides, I left home ages ago.

My auntie had to have a hip replacement, said Salma, spitting a pellet of chewing gum into her palm. NHS only gives you a couple of shitty physio sessions. My uncle went private, it was well expensive, but I can, like, give you the number, if you want it?

Thanks, I said. Fat chance, I thought, unless my mother had some gold bars squirrelled away somewhere along with her organic oil.

Can she, like, go to work, and stuff, if she can't walk? Salma asked, and I started to feel irritated.

Hip replacements are for old people, I said. Hers is her pelvis. It'll get better. She walks to work, to everywhere. She'll be fine.

*

Dying light as we made our way into the dusk of the woods. Sun splintering through the trees. I was on edge. Every step I took, something seemed to break, or move under my foot. Snap. Crunch. I jumped, every time.

What was that?

A squirrel's not going to let you step on it, chill out, he said over his shoulder. I crunched hard on something bony and soft. A snail?

What was that?

Here, he called, dropping to his knees. Knew I'd seen some, here.

He was kneeling by a fallen tree that looked like it had broken out in blisters: bright orange bubbling along its trunk Chanterelle, he said, rummaging on the ground. Tastes like apricot. You probably eat them all the time, don't you, mushrooms? Burger places use them as a meat replacement, because they're fibrous, like meat, and they soak up juices well.

Poisonous, aren't they? I asked. He shook his head.

Not as many as you'd think. Similar texture to an octopus, actually, but earthier, y'know. Kind of fruitier. So they're more usually used for meat than fish. D'you know that the meat of an animal that eats fruit and veg'll taste different to one that eats other animals?

I came and knelt too, resting my forearm on his back. I could feel the warm trunk of his body through his anorak, but I could not see his face, studying the mushroom.

Well, aren't you an encyclopaedia. What other foods are poisonous? I asked.

I felt rather than saw him shrug. Uncooked seafood, he said. Bad meat. Things that aren't broken-down enough, or broken-down too much.

His voice went flat, all of a sudden. Anything, if you let it rot, he said. Unless rotting's what makes it. Everything we eat's on a sliding scale, from smelly to furry. You've got your fur on blue cheese, the crust they scrape off your luxury dry-aged meat, your medlars, which are like rancid apples you let turn to brown mush. Tastes like vanilla custard. All ripe fruit, actually, is just one long slowed-down stage of decay. A peach should be brimming with liquor inside its skin, so it bruises if you all but breathe on it, and you've got to eat it over a sink because it spurts. Like a water balloon. Everything luxury – everything special – is just dying, but paused. Even when you make olives, you have to crush them, half-destroy them, then cure them; that is, pause the rotting, sort of. Everything is violent, with food, on its way to rot and back again. We eat rot, we eat death.

He was staring at the chanterelle like it was a severed head. I took my arm off his back. Are y'angry with me? I said.

He twisted round, surprised. You? he said.

I don't not-eat meat just because it grosses me out! I said, hearing my cold voice.

And at the same time as I knew that what I'd said was not entirely true, I knew that I was also not able to explain those sheep, and what they meant to me. There were no sheep like that when I escaped to Sheffield. Up here, the animals and everything else are backed into a dead end; their lives turning into scrag-ends. Trapped. Their blank, bleak gaze.

He looked at me, confused. My brother texted, he said, matter-of-factly. Asking something about, how's my meat-flavoured chewing-gum going. He says, it's disgusting. *It's not what normal people should eat*, blah, blah. The kind of crap baby-meat he'd like to make – tender? It bloody dissolves in your mouth! And it's expensive, he's conning the lads who work for him. Might as well pay good money for a fish finger, or a mushroom.

My rush of bravery had died down, as usual. I tried a lame smile. The world would be a better place if we were all on mushrooms, I said.

Everything is old, and dead! he said. Beer is mould and ferment, so's the pickled onions in the pub. Silverskins. Oysters, they filter the shit from the sea and people pay thirty quid for them in the cities. Fresh fish. It's fucked up, Star! It's like, there's this cult of freshness. As if the less time between it being alive and it being dead, the better. We're scared of death, Star! Of old age, and rot and decay, and we hide it! We lie about it.

I rocked back on my heels, silently agreeing. Meat: blood. A dead body. Something's final terror and pain, blooming on my tongue. He and I had the same hatred of lying, but we'd reached different conclusions. I looked at the earth.

He let out a sigh, knuckled his forehead.

What's wrong? I said.

Meggie died, he said, and I saw his shoulders slump the tiniest amount, his voice hollowing out. Just old age.

II.

I sit in my mother's empty house, that night. It sags around me, cardboard walls like old skin. I can hear something – mice, woodlice? – scritch-scratching along in the skirting boards. It is one of those flimsy post-war maisonettes built out of cardboard, and the wind whistles through the cracks she let widen. She half-heartedly whitewashed the kitchen and front room, when we first moved in, when she had all her idealistic dreams of living in the countryside. But whitewash just means the spiders show up more. I used to try to save them, later, when she was banging a broom in the corners and crying. *I* hate *this house! Nasty,* dirty *house!*

Silverfish in the sink. Dirt and grime building up in the corners like soil. The outside is coming in; the house is quietly seething with life, like a grave full of worms.

It's not a night we'd arranged to see each other. I text him. *busy tonight?* Then: *u around?* Then: *what's up?* Finally, I get: *sorry just got caught up. see you tmrw yeah?*

I go round early the next day, and have to bang on the door five times before I get let in. The first thing I notice is the cold air: stale and pooling around us. The second thing is his fear: shoulders hunched, shielding himself with the door, eyes skittering past me to search the yard beyond. I reach up to cup his face in my hands, and try to tug it down. I want to feel its warm, scratchy weight, so that it sweeps away the spongy feeling of my mother's cheek. I want him to tell me what he is going to cook for me tonight, that he will look after me for ever and ever, and that he will never, ever eat meat again.

But he gives an irritable little shake of the head and his beard scrapes through my fingertips. I reach up again, determined, and stand on tiptoe to press my mouth on his. He does not resist; I stick my tongue through and wiggle it in his mouth, screwing my eyes closed, tasting his spit, the familiar walls and muscles of his mouth, but it's only for a second and then his hands are on my shoulder, gently – always gently! He must kill gently, too – pushing me away. Star, he says. It's over.

*

We trudge up through the fields at the back of the farm, and stop at the top of the hill. Sure enough, over on the other side of the river, you can see a fenced field full of sheep, several battered Land Rovers placed at strategic points between. I can just make out a couple of figures leaning against one.

My brother's friends came down at night with their dogs, shifted the sheep, he says. I could do nothing. No Meggie – I ran out, but they had guns.

But you've got friends, too? I say, and he scoffs, kicking the earth.

I've got Johnno and Foster, two teenagers, and a couple of poshos at the shop who don't need to work for a living, he says. My brother's grown up farming here, while I fucked off to catering college. He's got the neighbours. My dad's old mates.

His hands are scraped across the knuckles, I notice, as though he has been punching something wooden. A door, a wardrobe, a kennel.

But I thought you owned everything on the farm, I say.

Only technically, he says. It's me that's the oldest. But my dad made his will years ago, before he knew I'd leave. My brother has a claim to those sheep because he bred 'em.

But I thought you were going to court – I say.

I've lost it all, Star, he says, his voice slow and sad. I need the supplier as backing, to prove I can make the farm work my way. The supplier's coming this week, to look at the sheep for his restaurants, and I've not got sheep. I'll have no time to find another like him to line up before the court case, if there even is another like him in the country, so I'll lose the case. They can claim I'm not caring for it as my father would have wished. I've no capital to buy more sheep. The farm shop I built – I took too many risks. It's swallowed up my savings. I've lost.

His voice stops, abruptly. Silence, for a second. Then a bird starts singing full-throatedly somewhere in the blue sky above.

You just need time, I say.

I'll win it if I can prove I can make a go of it, he says. His voice begins to spiral higher, like the birdsong. And if I lose this supplier, I won't.

He says something about going back to vegetable chopping in hotel basement kitchens. I watch the distant, ringed pack of sheep, encircled by squatting metal wolves. I feel weirdly calm, but at the same time my mind is tumbling with frantic calculations. I don't want to leave him. I don't want to see his shoulders slump, his voice turn false. Even if it meant sacrificing my principles – as she called them – does it matter, if I can save his? And if it'd help the sheep, anyway?

You've still got the house, for now, I say. The supplier doesn't need to know anything's changed. You need to show him an old animal, that you've butchered.

There's no farmer for miles around who'll sell to me, he says. Besides, the supplier knows what a young sheep looks like.

He won't know what cull yaw looks like, will he? I say.

He looks sideways at me through his long eyelashes, taking in my face, and I see something changing in his. For the first time, I feel like he's uncertain of me, rather than the other way round.

He won't be so familiar with it, no, he says.

You need an old animal, I say. Make use of something.

*

The kitchen is warm, and smells of coffee and the cool flesh of Meggie's body, which lies on the kitchen table peeled of skin like a banana. It seems rude to see her like this; I imagine myself flayed in the same way, modestly covering my veins and papillary lobes with the muscles of my hand. The green oilcloth is covered with a tarp. Laid out on that are: a boning knife, a small meat saw, a smaller, steel boning knife and a cleaver. We won't have time to hang it long, he says. And we'll hang it in the barn so he can't see too well.

He is all business, now that I've made the decision for us. His brow furrowed as he inspects the body. Dark enough, he says. Could pass as cull yaw, I'd reckon.

Looks like the fucking Stone Age in here, I say. He looks up, and studies my face for a second.

You OK?

Except in the Stone Age people mostly ate cracked grains and roots, actually, I say, and he shrugs as though he can't waste time trying to understand me, and turns back to Meggie's body. It doesn't look like Meggie, any more, and that's OK.

Dark meat, he says. That's good, looks right.

How did you know how to bleed it? I ask.

I saw them bleeding animals when I was at the butchers, once, he says. Boss took us to the abattoir. The lads there used to do things like put cows' tongues in each others' lunchboxes, as a joke.

Imagine it: clicking open the lid of your steel lunchbox, gaping at the purpling muscle flopped over your cheese-and-pickle sandwich. Sounds gurgling from the back of your throat as if your own tongue has been cut out.

Will you hold here? he asks. He is edging careful fingers around the loop of her rose-pink hip, pressing down.

What are you doing? I ask.

Gotta find the pelvic girdle.

The coffee and raw meat smell is making me nauseous, and the cornflakes I ate earlier are beginning to move lumpily around in my stomach. I steel myself as he slices into Meggie's pelvis. Be the knife, be as cold and hard as the knife. This is the only way. My mother's voice says, *I thought you couldn't even bear to work in a supermarket, Star, and look at you now!* His brow is deeply furrowed in concentration and I see that he has managed to separate Meggie, in his head, from this rose-petal pink and bruised body lying on the tarp in front of us. Be the knife. I breathe out through my mouth, flex my toes inside my trainers.

The saw scratches through her spine and she breaks in two on the table. Her poor ribs open to the air. One of his hands is inside her ribcage, now, tickling her darkest crevices, counting her ribs. She is an architecture of skin stretched over bone. Two, three, four, five, he says, and looks up to flash me a grin. All good! he says. You know, this might just work. Then he registers the look on my face, and his smile crumbles away, and he drops the pathetic thing he is holding – how could I have said this was making use of it? The thing that was once all scent of hot hair and hay seed, an elastic and panting weight in my arms – and comes towards me. And I can smell the cold blood on his hot hands, and scream out before he reaches me, to get him away.

*

The supplier laps up our lies, barely even glancing at the dark joints of Meggie where they lie arranged neatly in a shadowy corner of the barn. He talks to him smoothly about experimenting with salmon cuts and length of hanging time. *I believe it's best to know the meat myself, you know, though the abattoir does most of the butchery. I like to keep my hand in!*

I hang back, not saying a word. The supplier shoots me a couple of odd looks, but mostly addresses himself to him. I go back into the kitchen, and reheat a vegetarian shepherd's pie, but the potato is too much like sour cream, and sour cream too much like fat, and tiny lentils pool at the side of my plate like blind frog eyes. I get up, pick up my plate to scrape the food into the bin, but when I do, the whole plate slides in, gracefully and smoothly as though I had meant to drop it on purpose.

When he comes in, he is glowing after waving the supplier off. I tell him I have to leave. I have to visit my mother, I say.

*

A few days later. Why d'you keep breaking things? my mother asks, pulling her blankets up to her jowls. Bed is where she spends most of her time, now. Oh, *Star*.

Her breakfast tray lies smashed on the floor of her bedroom. I don't know how it slipped from my hands. I study the triangles and pentagons on the floor and announce that I will glue them back together; and I do, I buy superglue from Poundland and sit in the kitchen that night in the weak light of a single bulb and try to make them what they were before.

*

Another night. The twilight sky. I don't know what's wrong with you, my mother frets. My phone rings again, and I pull it out of my jeans to reject the call.

Nothing's wrong, I tell her, and tuck in the blankets; tugging them down viciously, pinning her in.

You're getting skinny, she says, tilting her head and watching me beadily over the top of the blanket. You've got to be careful. Men don't like skinny girls!

She bucks her pointed knees underneath the blanket, underneath where I am sitting, and I am pushed off sharply. I walk to the window and stare out into the dusk. Fragments of small houses in pools of sodium light. Potholes. The gloss of parked cars. A girl totters past, lights up a cigarette. A man wearing his army khakis steps smartly the other way. Blue of Sky Sports glowing through the window of the pub at the corner, a few blokes on spice already lolling wall-eyed on the pavement outside.

I want him so much. For a second, I can almost feel the heat of his body pressed against mine: the throb of his blood in his groin and the seawater of his breath. Hard to believe that I felt that, now.

I open my eyes and turn back to the bed. She lies there, a bag of fluids and splintering bones, her blue hands pawing restlessly at the blanket. What if we had killed her, instead of Meggie? I'd considered it, obviously, as we'd stood on the top of the hill and watched that metal encirclement, when the idea had first flashed through my panicking mind. She's no use to anybody alive. Nobody would notice her gone. It might even have worked; she'd got barely any more meat on her than a skinny old ewe.

And then, when I saw Meggie's stripped, humiliated body, I realised how easy it would have been. And that was what sent a slow, cold coil of terror unfurling down my spine: that it would've been so stupidly easy. That he and I could, actually, have thumped my mother on her head, and she'd have been suddenly nothing more than a lump of pink marble, rocking stupidly on the table as the world kept turning and he swore and sweated and I fetched him cups of tea. And I realised, those hands of his – the hands that revolted and fascinated me when I was a kid, the hands that were blood and dirt and death all sickeningly rolled together with feeling and desire – the same violence was in my hands, too.

I'm guilty, whether I did it or not. Once I'd seen Meggie's bare body, and realised that, I couldn't lie to myself any more. And so that was why I had to leave him, and go back to her, and pay for it; by caring for her and keeping her alive.

I can always smell Meggie's body on my fingertips, no matter how many rollies I smoke before I brush my teeth in the morning; no matter how I scrub with Pears and Dove and carbolic, digging into the nail bed and peeling cuticles. I walk up and down the soap aisle in the supermarket where I work now, inspecting handpumps and shower gels, and I buy nail scrubbers and brush my hands till they look corrugated and purple as a steak, prickling with beads of blood. I see my colleagues' faces twist when they look at me.

I'm not running off with any men, I say aloud, now, to the rumpled bed. Each word feels like a rock, falling from my mouth to bury me. I'll be here forever, I say. I'll take care of you.

Acknowledgements

Advice on emotional and physical abuse can be found at: www.refuge.org.uk

My thanks first and foremost to Aaron Kent and the Broken Sleep team, who put so much work and thought into this and every one of their projects, and are both professional and kind.

Thanks to Alice and Aileen, who gave feedback on an earlier version of 'Offlanders'.

Thanks to Miruna and Oliver, for reading faster than I ever could have expected.

Thanks to Daisy and Georgia, for seeing the original dog in the woods and planting the seed in my mind.

This book is for my father, who counts sheep.

LAY OUT YOUR UNREST